Happy Reading

Ommie + Ce

FLAT STANLEY's
ADVENTURES IN CLASSROOM 2E

Catch Flat Stanley's Worldwide Adventures:

Riding the Slides

Created by **Jeff Brown**

Written by **Kate Egan**

Pictures by **Nadja Sarell**

HARPER

An Imprint of HarperCollinsPublishers

Library of Congress Control Number: 2023932490
ISBN 978-0-06-309501-4 (hardcover) — 978-0-06-309500-7
(paperback)

Typography by Laura Mock
23 24 25 26 27   PC/CWR   10 9 8 7 6 5 4 3 2 1

First Edition

For my real-life slide testers,
Ellory and Rowenna

Contents

Jumping Contest

The school day was just starting, and Stanley Lambchop was sitting at his classroom desk. Or, really, he was *trying* to sit at his desk.

"Let's settle down and stay in our chairs, friends," said his second-grade teacher, Ms. Root. She was speaking to the whole class, but Stanley had a feeling this message was for him.

"I'm doing my best!" he said. He

scooted back in his chair until he was sitting up straight.

The teacher smiled. "Just a helpful reminder."

Ms. Root never raised her voice when her students made mistakes—she just gave them helpful reminders. But Stanley Lambchop got more helpful reminders than most of his classmates.

That was because Stanley was not like any of the other second graders. One day, not that long ago, a bulletin board had fallen off the wall in his bedroom. It landed right on top of Stanley, and it left him as flat as a pancake!

Stanley had lots of adventures

because he was flat. He had traveled around the world, from Mexico to China, and had met lots of people and friends along the way. Flatness had even made him famous!

The problem was that pancakes weren't *only* flat.

They were also smooth, and sometimes it was hard for two smooth things to stick together.

Two smooth things like, for instance, Stanley Lambchop and his chair.

If Stanley did not hold on, he would slip right out of his chair and onto the floor! He had a hard time sitting still because he was always trying to fix his position.

Now Stanley settled into a new spot. He braced his legs under the desk while Ms. Root called out names for attendance. The school year was still new, but Stanley was getting to know the routine.

Ms. Root went down her class list

in alphabetical order. Stanley paid extra attention as she got closer to his name.

"Elena?" said Ms. Root.

Elena, Stanley's classmate, put her hand up so fast it was a blur. Elena did *everything* fast.

Ms. Root smiled and continued. "Evan?"

Just like every morning, Evan was looking out the window.

Ms. Root waited until he noticed his name had been called. "Oh, sorry!" Evan said. "Yes, I'm here!"

Josie was next. "I'm here today, too," Josie said clearly. Her pencils were in a neat row on her desk.

"Juniper?" said Ms. Root.

"Present," said Juniper.

Every morning, at least one of the kids said "present" instead of "here." It never stopped being funny! Everyone giggled before Ms. Root went on.

Soon she came to Marco, Stanley's best friend. "Here!" Marco said when his name was called. "Just wondering—what's for lunch today?"

Ms. Root put her hand up. "In a minute, friend," she said. "Let's finish our first task of the day." Even when kids were doing things she did not like, Ms. Root always called them "friend."

Stanley's name was next. "Oh, I already know Stanley is here," said Ms. Root, smiling.

"Sophia?" she said. Sophia gave a wave from her wheelchair.

"And Stevie," Ms. Root finished.

Stevie piped up from the back of the room. "Here!" he said. Stevie's voice was as small as he was.

Now the school day could begin!

Ms. Root began the morning with a song and some stretches. Then the class practiced adding numbers. A little later, they had art.

Whenever Stanley felt himself slipping, he pulled himself right back up in his chair. He did not want to slump for his favorite part of the morning. When it was finally time for read-aloud, Stanley was ready!

"Who would like to help me turn

the pages today?" Ms. Root asked the class.

Stanley's hand shot up. He waved it wildly in the air. There was no way to miss it! But Ms. Root's eyes skipped over him. She chose Josie to help instead.

Josie pushed up her glasses and went to stand beside the teacher.

Stanley sighed. He looked at Marco, who was sitting next to him.

"Not again!" whispered Marco.

"Ms. Root picks her all the time!" Stanley whispered back.

Ms. Root opened her book and started reading.

The story was about a girl who asked a lot of questions. She wanted to learn about everything!

Stanley's teacher pointed to a long word in the story. "*Inquire*," she said. "Does anyone know what that means?"

The whole class was quiet until Josie raised her hand.

"I do!" said Josie. "I think *inquire* means to ask."

Marco whispered to Stanley again. "Is there anything Josie doesn't know?" he asked.

Marco was right, Stanley thought. Josie was supersmart. She never even got any helpful reminders! He wondered how she did it.

He was still wondering when read-aloud was over. "We'll leave it there for today, friends," Ms. Root said, closing the book.

"Awwww!" the kids said. But then it was time for something just as good as read-aloud. It was time for recess!

Stanley and his classmates stood up, found their jackets, and stood in a line. They walked quietly out of the classroom, down the hallway, and through the doors. Then they burst onto the playground!

It was a crisp, cool morning at Maple Shade Elementary. The school was surrounded by tall trees, and their leaves were golden against a clear blue sky. The red brick of the building glowed in the sunshine.

Ms. Root's class scattered across the

playground. Evan went to the swings, Josie played hopscotch, and Juniper climbed on the big dome in the middle of the grass. "I call the slide!" shouted Elena, dashing toward it. Sophia and Stevie played catch.

"Hey, Stanley! Try to catch me!" Marco called out. He raced over to the monkey bars and scrambled up a ladder. Before Stanley could climb up after him, Marco was swinging across a long row of bars, hand over hand.

"Here I come!" Stanley took a deep breath and followed his friend. He tried to go fast! But Stanley's hands started to hurt. Then his arms started to ache!

How did monkeys do this? Stanley wondered.

It took him a while, but somehow he managed to make it to the other side, where Marco was waiting.

"Woo-hoo!" Stanley said, high-fiving Marco. "I did it!"

"Woo-hoo!" Marco replied.

Then there was *another* woo-hoo from the far end of the playground. "What's going on over there?" Marco asked.

"Let's go take a look!" Stanley replied. They ran over to the swings.

A minute ago, only Evan was there. Now Josie and Juniper were side by side, pumping their legs as hard as they could. A group had gathered to watch, and Stanley and Marco joined them.

"It's a swinging contest!" Elena told the boys. "Right now, Juniper is winning."

Juniper was daring and loud. Her ponytail flew out behind her as she swung. "Can't catch me!" she yelled.

"This could be dangerous," warned Stevie. He was not a fan of taking risks.

Josie leaned back in her swing and pumped extra hard. She was out of breath, but she was swinging high and gaining speed. Soon she was even with Juniper!

"So who's higher now?" Juniper

called to Marco, who was still on the ground.

"I can't really tell," Marco admitted. "I think it might be a tie."

"Hmm," said Juniper. "Do you know how to jump off a swing?" she asked Josie.

"I don't think that's a good idea . . ." Stevie cautioned.

Josie ignored him. "Sure, I can jump," she said. "Want to see who can go farthest?"

"Yes!" said Juniper. Now it was a jumping contest!

Juniper got her swing going pretty high, then she let go and sailed through the air. She landed in some soft wood chips near the edge of the swing area.

But Josie went even farther. She landed just where the playground's wood chips met the pavement, right in the middle of someone else's hopscotch game! Stevie covered his eyes.

Marco looked at Stanley. Stanley looked at Marco.

They both wanted to try, too!

"Hey, can I have a chance?" Stanley asked Josie.

Stevie backed away at once. "Not me!" he said. "I don't want a chance."

But Elena stepped right up. "Okay, Stanley Lambchop, I challenge you to a jumping contest! Whoever wins will face off against Josie."

"You're on!"

In no time, Stanley and Elena were side by side on the swings. Stanley pumped hard to make the swing go both fast and high. He was watching Elena, and Elena was watching him.

When the swings drew about even, Elena took a flying leap. She landed in the same place as Juniper.

Stanley swung back one more time. Then, as his swing came forward, he pushed off and jumped!

Beneath him, he could see the wood chips, the pavement, the hopscotch, and . . . the climbing dome? The school's brick walls coming toward him?

"Noooooo!" cried Stevie.

Suddenly, Stanley realized he had caught a breeze. He wasn't just jumping now. He was soaring above the playground like a kite!

Wind swept up some of the dried leaves on the playground, spinning them in circles. Stanley went in circles, too! By the time he landed, he was pretty dizzy. But no one would ever be able to jump so far. Stanley was all the way on the other side of the school!

His classmates crowded around him, cheering.

Marco pumped his fist in the air. "Awesome!" he said. "No one can ever beat that!"

Elena gave him a high five. "I think you set a new record for the Maple Shade Elementary playground," she said.

But Josie shook her head. "I think we need a do-over," she said. "That was no fair."

Scientists

Stanley was still thinking about his win—and Josie's disappointment—when he got back into the classroom.

"A do-over?" he whispered to Marco. "No way!"

"You couldn't help flying," Marco pointed out.

"I know!" said Stanley. "Just like I can't help being flat!"

"Maybe Josie doesn't like to be

second place," his friend said.

"Shhhh," said Stanley. That might be true, he thought. But Ms. Root was starting her lesson!

The teacher cleared her throat and looked around the room. When everyone was quiet, she said, "I have a big announcement to make, friends. Today we will be starting something new. Something we will work on together all year!"

She gathered the kids into a circle on the rug. "Welcome, scientists," she said.

Stanley and Marco looked around. They did not see any scientists.

Stanley raised his hand.

"Yes, Stanley?" said Ms. Root.

"Where are they?" Stanley asked. "The scientists, I mean?"

He was looking for people with clipboards and long white coats. He was looking for people with high-tech tools.

"Good question. *You* are the scientists!" said Ms. Root, waving her hand around the circle. "Everyone in this class is a scientist."

"Oh, I don't think so," Stevie said. He shook his head firmly. "Kids are not scientists."

Ms. Root did not even give Stevie a helpful reminder about raising his hand. Sometimes she got so excited about something that the rules went out the window.

"Ah, that's where you are wrong!"

She clapped her hands together. "*Anyone* can be a scientist!" Ms. Root exclaimed. "Did you learn about plants in first grade?"

Stanley and his classmates nodded. First grade seemed like a long time ago now.

"We planted some seeds," Juniper said.

"We watched them grow," Marco remembered.

"We kept a class journal," added Elena.

"That was science!" cried Ms. Root. "Observing, exploring, *inquiring*—or asking questions—these things are all a part of science!"

Juniper shook her head. "We

observe and explore all the time," she said. "Does that mean we are doing science all the time?"

"I don't think that's real science," said Josie. "Is it?" She looked at their teacher.

"Actually . . ." Ms. Root's eyes sparkled. "It *is* real science, I promise," she told her class. "And we are going to do it ourselves! We don't need a special lab or special tools. All we need is this!"

She turned to the whiteboard and wrote down one thing. It was a big question mark.

She faced the class, grinning. "Stanley, do you have questions?" she asked him.

"Um, yes," Stanley said. "I have questions about your question!"

Ms. Root laughed. "I mean, in your life. Do you ever want to know how or why things work?" she asked.

"Sure . . ." Stanley said.

"Any time you ask a question about the world around you, any time you try things out, you are doing what scientists do," Ms. Root promised, pointing to the board. "Without even realizing it, you might be using the *scientific method*!"

She looked around the room. "Can anyone tell me what that is?"

No one raised their hand because no one knew the answer.

"Well," said Ms. Root, "let me tell

you all about it!"

The kids in the circle leaned in as Ms. Root started to talk. Stanley could feel her excitement spreading around the room.

"Scientists watch everything very closely," said Ms. Root. "They watch, they listen, they touch and smell. They pay attention! But they do not always understand what they see. And so . . ."

She waited for someone to finish her sentence.

Marco raised his hand. "And so . . . they ask questions?"

"That's correct!" said Ms. Root, giving him a fist bump. Stanley gave his friend a fist bump, too.

Ms. Root continued. "Scientists

ask questions like why, and how, and when. And the scientific method is their special way of finding answers."

She stopped for a minute and gave a warning. "Now . . . stick with me. There are going to be some big words."

Ms. Root moved toward the board. "The first thing a scientist does to answer a question is to make a guess."

"A guess?" asked Marco. "That doesn't sound very scientific."

"Their *best* guess," said Ms. Root. "Based on what they have seen already. It is called a *hypothesis*."

She wrote it on the board and said it slowly out loud. "*High—pah—the—siss*. It might not be the scientist's final answer, but it is a place to start.

And then? Can anyone tell me what happens next?"

Juniper almost jumped out of her seat. "Yes! I can!" she said. "I think scientists . . . run some tests," she said. "They try things out. To see if their guess is right."

"Exactly!" said Ms. Root. "They run some tests. Another way to say that is they do *experiments*."

"Oh!" said Stanley. Everyone had heard of experiments.

Ms. Root wrote the word on the board, anyway. "That is the second step in the scientific method," she said. "Testing the hypothesis. Experimenting to find the answer."

She looked around the room.

"Everyone with me so far?"

When everyone nodded, Ms. Root went on. "Okay! The next step is to make a *conclusion*," she said. "That is basically a big decision."

Stevie frowned. "Isn't a conclusion an ending?" he said.

Ms. Root nodded. "It is an ending, yes. The end of the scientific method, you could say. But it is more than that, too."

She looked around to make sure everyone was listening. "The conclusion tells us what the experiments have shown. It tells us if the hypothesis was right or wrong!"

"So," said Ms. Root. She paused dramatically. "We will be doing some science together in this very room! We will be making a hypothesis, doing some experiments, and drawing our own conclusions. We will be going through the scientific method from top to bottom! Who can't wait to get started?"

The kids all started talking at once. "Me! Me! I can't wait to get started!" they all said. Ms. Root knew how to get her class fired up.

Once the uproar died down, Ms. Root said, "We will also be adding some steps of our own . . ."

Stevie's hand shot up. "Is that what real scientists do?" he asked. "Add their own steps?"

Ms. Root smiled. "Like I said, we

are all real scientists in this class-room," she said. "But we are also learning. We are learning how to think in a scientific way. The steps we add to the scientific method will make our science extra fun. And yes, real scientists love to have fun!"

Josie was writing everything down. "So what are the extra steps?" she asked. Her pencil was ready to go.

Ms. Root said, "They are just a few things to remember along the way."

She wrote them on the board in capital letters, so Stanley knew they were extra important.

- NO QUESTION IS A BAD QUESTION.
- BE PATIENT.

- OBSERVE CAREFULLY, AND RECORD
WHAT YOU SEE.
- NEVER BE AFRAID TO MAKE A MESS.
- EXPECT SURPRISES!

Stanley Lambchop loved surprises!

He looked at Marco, and they both grinned. He had a feeling they were going to love science, too.

Stanley vs. Arthur

For homework, Ms. Root's students were supposed to come up with questions to answer with the scientific method. Stanley didn't have a question yet, but Ms. Root said not to worry.

"Questions come up all the time," she promised him. So Stanley waited.

In the meantime, he was also waiting in a line at the edge of the playground. Any minute now, the school bus would arrive to take him home.

Stanley dropped his backpack off in his bus line. Then he looked for his younger brother, Arthur.

"What's going on? Where's the bus?" Arthur grumbled when he arrived. He could never wait to get

home after school. He could never wait to eat his after-school snack!

"That's what everyone wants to know!" Stanley said.

From the line next to him, Marco added, "My bus is late, too!"

Just then, a teacher named Mr. Collins spoke up. "May I have your attention please?" he said to the kids in the bus lines. "I have an update."

He raised his voice and said, "I'm afraid I have some bad news."

"Bad news" was all it took to make the students listen.

"Bad news" made Stevie look pretty worried.

"Due to heavy traffic," Mr. Collins said, "all the buses will be delayed.

You may leave your bags in line and proceed to the playground. When the bell rings, you will need to return to your lines."

If he had anything else to add, his voice was drowned out by the roar of kids with extra time to play.

Arthur turned to Stanley. "Guess we'll have to shoot some hoops!" he said.

The Lambchop boys were into basketball these days. They had a hoop in their driveway at home, and they were always playing.

Stanley followed his brother to a big bin of playground balls. Arthur dug into the bin for a bright orange basketball.

"Catch!" he said, flinging it in Stanley's direction. Stanley caught the ball and dribbled it across the playground until he got to the basketball hoop. He shot the ball, but he missed.

"Awww, too bad!" said Arthur, coming up behind him. Stanley ran off with the ball, but Arthur stole it. He dribbled to the other side of the hoop, did some fancy footwork, and made his own shot. *Swish!* Arthur had a basket!

Stanley caught the rebound, bounced the ball quickly, and tried again. The ball rolled around the rim of the basket. It looked like it was going to go in! At the last minute, though, it fell toward the pavement.

"Next time!" Arthur said, encouraging Stanley.

Then Arthur's best friends, Nate and Jaden, ran toward the brothers.

"My ball!" Nate called out, and Arthur tossed it to him. Nate stood in one spot, dribbling slowly, until he made a shot from halfway across the playground. If this were a real game, it would have been a three-pointer!

"Nice!" said Arthur.

Luckily, Marco decided to join Stanley's team. Now it was three against two!

Marco rushed in for a rebound, but Jaden beat him to it.

Stanley stuck with Jaden as he

dribbled it all over the place, but the ball was always just out of reach. Stanley and Marco were not quite fast enough to steal it back.

Juniper, Stanley's classmate, was watching from her bus line. "You've got this, Stanley!" she yelled. "You've got this, Marco!"

Stanley and Marco kept on shooting. After a while, though, Stanley realized that they were not playing very well. And everyone was watching! He wished they could keep up with Arthur and his friends. He wished the younger boys were not so quick!

When Marco passed the ball, Stanley caught it and hurled it toward the basket. Maybe it would go in this time? No. Stanley let out a sigh.

Then he had a stroke of good luck. The younger boys were guarding him as he dribbled toward the basket. He could hardly see past them. But Stanley was as flat as a piece of paper! He slipped right between Nate and Jaden and leaped into the air. Stanley dunked and scored!

"Yes, Stanley!" Marco cheered.

"Way to go!" Juniper chimed in.

When the bell rang, Stanley and Marco were one basket ahead of the first-grade boys! Stanley high-fived Marco and said, "We're a good team!"

The buses began to arrive in a long yellow row, and the kids quickly

scattered to their different lines. It was time to go home.

Stanley clutched his seat tightly on the bus. He did not want to slide into his brother when the bus went over a bump. Why were the bus seats so slippery? Stanley wondered. Was that a question he could answer with the scientific method? Maybe not, he decided.

He was still thinking about his assignment when he arrived home. Stanley left his backpack in the mud room, but he kept one notebook in his hand. That way he could write down any good ideas that came to him. He was bound to have one any minute now.

"How was your day?" asked Mr. Lambchop, who was working from home.

"It was good!" said Stanley. He told his father about the jumping contest and the scientific method. "Do you know what it means to *inquire*?" he asked.

Arthur interrupted with a different question. "What's for snack?" he asked their father.

Arthur had a stack of cookies, plus a peanut butter and banana sandwich and a tall glass of milk. When he was all done, he wanted to know when they were having dinner!

After he ate, Arthur went to his room, but Stanley stayed downstairs with his father. Mr. Lambchop cut vegetables for his famous spaghetti sauce while Stanley sat at the kitchen table with his notebook.

"I need to answer a scientific question," he told his dad. "But I don't know what it should be."

"Ah! Well . . ." Mr. Lambchop started. He was always full of ideas. "The kitchen is an excellent place for observation," he said. "When I cook these vegetables for a long time, they break down into my spaghetti sauce. It's science at work!"

"Hmm," said Stanley. "Interesting. But I think I like eating more than I like cooking."

It was getting dark when his

mother got home from her office. She tried to help Stanley, also. "Maybe you could ask a question about the moon or the stars?" she suggested.

But Stanley wasn't sure how he could answer a question like that. He might need a telescope or something.

Soon Mrs. Lambchop set the table for dinner, and Mr. Lambchop served the spaghetti. The whole family ate together, like most nights. And, like most nights, Mrs. Lambchop wanted to know all the news from school.

"I learned that I was a scientist," Stanley told his mother.

"My class is taking a test tomorrow," Arthur said.

"We played basketball together

after school!" Stanley said. "It was me and Marco against Arthur and his friends. And we won!"

"Well . . ." said Arthur. "Sort of."

"Wait, what?" sputtered Stanley. "What do you mean?"

Arthur swallowed his bite of spaghetti. "I just mean that I don't want you to play with my friends again. Unless you agree not to cheat."

Stanley stood up. "Cheat?!" he said. He put his hands on his hips. "I did not cheat!" he told his brother.

"You used your flatness, and you don't think that's cheating?" Arthur retorted.

"Boys!" said Mr. Lambchop. "That's enough. Let's just cool down a little . . ."

The brothers kept arguing. "I can't help being flat, okay?" Stanley said.

"But you can help taking advantage of it," Arthur said. "You shouldn't get to do things no one else can do."

Stanley did not think he could win

this argument. But he could not finish his dinner, either. "May I please be excused?" he asked his parents, using his best manners. Then he went to his room to think. Was it really true?

Sometimes flatness helped him, sure. Josie had noticed, and Arthur had noticed, too. But how was he supposed to stop it? Stanley didn't think he should be called a cheater just for being who he was.

Not Again!

In school the next day, Stanley's classmates shared their scientific questions. While Ms. Root called on each friend, Stanley crumpled into his chair. Everybody else had such great ideas! It had taken him a long time to come up with a question. Now he did not want to tell anyone what it was.

Ms. Root was writing everything on the board. "I have never seen such great questions from a second-grade class!" she said with excitement. "I *knew* you were all scientists!"

Lots of kids had their hands up, so Stanley put his hand down for now.

The teacher called on Sophia. Softly, Sophia said, "My science question comes from my garden. I want to know how bees help flowers grow."

"Excellent question!" Ms. Root said. She added it to her list.

"Ooh! Ooh! Me next!" Marco called out, stretching his arm up as far as it would go.

"Yes, friend," Ms. Root said. "What's on your mind, Marco?"

"I want to know how water turns into ice," he said.

"Yes!" said Ms. Root, punching the air. "Another great question to explore. Who's next?" Ms. Root looked around. "Josie?"

Josie pushed up her glasses. She said, "My question is, why is it so important for us to wash our hands?"

Stanley and Marco looked at each other. That was a question only a grown-up could love.

Sure enough, Ms. Root clapped with delight. "Oh, yes! Studying germs is very important!"

Stanley was still nervous about his idea. His question was about bones. The question had come to him when he spotted a Halloween decoration in his window at home. It was a skeleton! Stanley wondered: How did all those bones stick together in a body? Fake skeletons had wires or threads connecting the bones. But what about in real life?

Now he did not want to say it out loud. What if the other kids laughed at him? Did they all know the answer already? They probably did, he thought.

And someone might say something about *his* bones, too. Were they flat, like the rest of him? Stanley wasn't sure. And how would he use the scientific method to answer his question, anyway?

Stanley stayed quiet for a long time as all his classmates continued to talk.

Finally, Ms. Root said, "Now, who has not had a turn?" There were only a few kids left, but Ms. Root did not get to all of them. By the time recess rolled around, Stanley still hadn't shared. He took a deep breath as he lined up with his class.

When they got outside, Josie had a great idea for a game. "Who wants to play freeze tag?" she called out. Soon the kids in Ms. Root's class were spreading out across the playground.

"I'll be it," Josie shouted. She closed her eyes and started counting.

"Come on!" Marco said to Stanley,

pointing to the climbing dome. They did not want to be the first people Josie froze!

"Three, two, one!" Josie said. "Ready or not, here I come!"

Even though Elena was a fast runner, Josie went after her right away.

She chased Elena over the wood chips and around the swings. She chased her over the dome and even down the slide!

"Got you!" Josie said when she finally tagged Elena.

"Wow," said Juniper. "I didn't think anyone could run faster than Elena!"

Elena was frozen in one place now. Stanley gave her a signal that he would try to free her. He would have

to sneak past Josie, but he was ready to do it. At least, he was ready until Josie started talking about him.

"I outran her fair and square," Josie said. "Not like that swinging and jumping contest. That wasn't fair at all, remember? When the rest of us were jumping, Stanley Lambchop was flying!"

Stanley scowled. "Josie is still mad about that," Marco whispered.

Stanley shook his head. He couldn't believe she was bringing this up again.

He didn't say anything because he wanted to unfreeze Elena. But it bothered him through the rest of recess. It bothered him when they went back into the classroom, too. All of a sudden, everyone seemed to think he was a cheater. All of a sudden, Stanley Lambchop was having a hard day.

As they all returned to their desks, Stanley was still thinking about what Josie said. And he was so distracted that he stopped paying attention to Ms. Root. She called on him to read something out loud, and Stanley had to admit he did not know what he was supposed to read. "Where are we again?" he asked. His face turned bright red.

"I have a helpful reminder for you, Stanley," Ms. Root said gently. "Try to stay with the class."

Later that day, Ms. Root came

up to Stanley's desk. "Do you have a minute?" she asked. Stanley nodded. Ms. Root spoke to him while the other kids were working.

"Is everything okay?" the teacher asked. "You've been very quiet today. Do you need to talk about anything?"

Stanley's face turned red all over again. "I don't know," he stammered.

"Is something bothering you?" Ms. Root asked. Her face was superserious, but also supernice.

Stanley decided he could tell her. "Yes, something is bothering me," he admitted. "And it is something I cannot change."

Now that he had started talking, he couldn't stop.

First, Stanley told Ms. Root his question about bones. "I did not want to share it with the class," he said. "I was worried that someone would answer it for me. Or make fun of me!"

Ms. Root shook her head. "That's not how good friends act," she said.

"Well, that's not all!" Stanley said.

Then he told his teacher about the contest on the playground. "We were trying to see who could jump the farthest off a swing," he explained. "Josie jumped really far. But I jumped farther because, well . . . I flew."

Ms. Root was confused. "You flew?" she asked.

"On a gust of wind," Stanley explained. "And Josie said I cheated! She keeps bringing it up, no matter what kind of contest we have."

"You've had other contests?" Ms. Root asked.

"Well, not yet," Stanley admitted. "I don't know if being flat would help me in other contests, but Josie sure thinks it would. She thinks I can win anything I want. And that's not all, Ms. Root! Do you want to know what's even worse? My younger brother agrees with her!"

Ms. Root thought that over. Then she stood up straight. Her eyes were bright.

"This, Stanley, is a question we can answer with the scientific method!" Ms. Root said. She broke into a little round of applause for her great idea.

"Um . . . really?" said Stanley.

They were not even talking about science. They were talking about recess!

But Ms. Root looked like she had discovered something big.

She said, "Don't you see? This

question is important to our whole class. Everybody wants playground games to be fair. And this question is also important to you, of course!"

"I don't understand . . ." Stanley said.

"You can study flatness!" exclaimed Ms. Root. "You can ask a question about it! How does flatness affect you on the playground?"

"I don't know," Stanley mumbled. He was not as excited as his teacher, but it was hard to say no to her. She was practically dancing around the classroom!

It was only that night, when he was talking to his mom after dinner, that he realized this was the perfect question after all. Mrs. Lambchop beamed, just like Ms. Root.

"This is perfect, Stanley," she pointed out. "If you study this question, you might also stop people from questioning when you win."

Observe and Record

The next morning, Ms. Root gathered her class back together on the rug. "Friends," she said, "we have an exciting change in plans!" She made it sound like they had just won a big prize, or they were about to leave for a fancy vacation.

"Now, I know you remember some of the extra steps we are adding to the scientific method," she said.

"No question is a bad question," Elena remembered.

"Make a mess?" Stevie said.

"Expect surprises!" Juniper called out.

"Yes!" Ms. Root beamed. "That's right!" she said. "And I have a surprise for the class today."

She lowered her voice dramatically. "We were going to begin with those questions you wrote for homework," she said. "Instead, we will begin exploring the scientific method *together*."

Ms. Root looked right at Stanley. "We have a Very Important Scientist in our classroom today. That person is Stanley Lambchop!"

Sophia's eyes opened wide. "Stanley?" she asked. "Why is he so important?"

"Well, as it happens," Ms. Root said, "Stanley has brought us a scientific question from real life! From *his* life. And some great scientific discoveries have come from real-world problems."

Stanley did not always like standing out because he was flat. Once in a while, he wished he was like the other kids. Today, though, he was excited to have a starring role.

Ms. Root continued, "Now . . . we've all seen what Stanley can do on the playground . . ."

Marco cut in. "He jumped to the

other side of the school!" he remembered.

"Which no one else could do," Josie
added.

Ms. Root put a hand up to stop her.
"He was putting his special quality—
his flatness—to work. *But is flatness
always the way to win? That is what
we need to know!*"

Juniper shook her head. "I think
we know the answer to that question
already," she said.

"But do we?" Ms. Root asked. "One
jumping contest might not be the
whole story, friends."

Ms. Root swept her hand around
the room, as if she was drawing a
circle that included everyone. "We,

together, can help Stanley Lambchop answer this question! We will use the scientific method. And maybe we will make recess just a little more peaceful, too."

Next to Stanley, Marco was muttering. "Let's hope so!" he said under his breath.

A hypothesis, Ms. Root reminded the class, was a prediction you made after observing something carefully. Once you made a prediction, you could test it with experiments.

"But before we get to any of that, we must observe," she said. "We must watch flatness in action on the playground!"

Stanley had been quiet, but now

he raised his hand.

"The question is really . . . big," he pointed out. Was it too big? he thought. "I mean . . . there is a lot to know about flatness . . ."

Rather than answering, Ms. Root sent the discussion right back to her students. "So how can we fix that?" she asked.

"Make the question smaller?" Evan said uncertainly. Sometimes he stared out the window, but he was definitely paying attention today.

"Yes!" Ms. Root cried out. "Let's just look at how flatness works on one part of the playground," she said.

Right away, Stanley said, "What about the slide?" No one thought he was a cheater on the slide—at least, not yet. He had no idea how flatness would help him or hurt him on the slide.

"Yes, that's perfect!" said Ms. Root, as happy as if it had been her own idea. She put the question a different way now and wrote it on the board: "Is flatness always the way to win on the slide?"

"Now, you may think you know all about the slide already, but today we are going to see it with new eyes," she went on.

She really meant new eyes! The first thing the class did was make funny glasses out of pipe cleaners. Ms. Root's new glasses were almost

as big as her face, and they were in every color of the rainbow! Stanley's were small and round.

"Do we really need to wear these?" asked Stevie, putting his glasses on top of his head.

"We are looking for details we have not noticed before, friends," Ms. Root told him. "These glasses will help us observe the playground slide in a whole new way!"

While the kids made their glasses, Ms. Root gathered a random collection of stuff from all around the classroom.

In a big box, Ms. Root had packed a textbook, a shiny zip-up pencil case, a roll of plastic wrap, some spray bottles filled with water, a towel, some clipboards, and a stopwatch.

Then, when everyone was ready, Stanley and Marco helped to carry this extra equipment. Everybody trooped outside, scattering leaves across the playground. It was funny to be outside without the rest of the second grade. Stanley kept forgetting that this wasn't recess. This was scientific work!

Another funny thing was that Ms. Root herself climbed to the top of the slide! In the sun, her glasses glittered.

"Our first job is to observe," Ms. Root explained to the class. "What do we notice when we send these flat objects down the slide? Our observations will lead us to a hypothesis."

She set the book on the top of one slide. Elena climbed up next to the teacher and set the pencil case on the top of another slide, right next to the first one. The other slide was exactly the same height and length.

"Now, imagine the book and the

pencil case are having a race," Ms. Root said. "What do you think is going to happen?"

Josie predicted, "The book will go faster because it's heavier."

Stanley whispered to Marco, "What does weight have to do with anything?" Marco shrugged. But if anyone had a different guess, they didn't say.

So Elena said, "Ready, set . . . go!" and she and Ms. Root let their items slide at the same time. Juniper clicked the watch when each thing landed.

"Oh!" said Josie, surprised. "The pencil case was faster. Hmm."

Stanley and Marco looked at each other. Maybe she would see things in

a new way after all.

Evan and Stevie were holding the clipboards.

"We need to write everything down," Stevie remembered. "Observe and record," he reminded everyone. Carefully, he took some notes.

"Now let's change things up a little," said Ms. Root, still on top of the slide. She wrapped the pencil case in a piece of plastic wrap. "Anyone want to guess what will happen now?" she asked.

Sophia rolled up to the end of the slide in her wheelchair. She peered at the pencil case. "I think the book will go faster," she said. "Because the pencil case is, like, sticky. It won't slide smoothly."

And she was right! The pencil case was still lighter than the book, but now it got stuck halfway down the slide. The plastic wrap seemed to slow it down.

Stevie scribbled more notes on his clipboard. Then Ms. Root said, "Let's observe one more condition before we come up with a hypothesis. What if we spray both slides with water?"

"That will make them water-slides!" Evan said. He handed a spray bottle to Stanley, and the two boys squirted the slides until they were soaked.

"Would anyone like to guess what will happen?" Ms. Root asked the class.

"I went to a water park last summer," Stanley said. "The waterslides were superfast!!"

"I think the book and the pencil case will both zoom," Marco added. "Maybe it will be a tie?"

It turned out the boys were both right and wrong. Ms. Root and Elena sent the items down the slide again. Then Juniper clicked the stopwatch and shared the results with the class.

"They both went faster than they went without the water," she announced. "But the pencil case won by a tenth of a second."

"Well, it was *almost* a tie," Marco said.

Stanley was not sure what any of

this had to do with their class science project. Or with flatness.

Luckily, Ms. Root was way ahead of the kids. "I think we have gathered some important information," she said. "Let's review our facts inside."

Stanley and Marco mopped up the slides with the towel. By the time they were finished, the towel was muddy and gray, but Marco just laughed.

"Well, Ms. Root said we could make a mess!" he said. Then the boys followed the rest of the kids back into their classroom.

Slide-off!

Ms. Root went over the findings with the kids. The pencil case was faster than the book, even when it was wet. But if it was wrapped in plastic, the pencil case lagged behind.

"Now, the next step will be not just to send flat things down the slide," Ms. Root said. "We will send a flat person!" Her excitement was contagious.

Marco punched the air. "Go Stanley!" he said.

"I'm ready!" Stanley announced. And he was!

Before they went home, Ms. Root gave them an assignment for tomorrow. "Now, we will need to make a prediction before Stanley goes down the slide. We have seen how flat objects behave on the slide. We have seen them race each other. What do you think will happen when a flat kid slides? What do you think will happen when he slides beside a not-flat kid?"

Stanley was not sure what would happen. Had he ever raced someone on the slides?

Arthur might remember, he thought. He decided he would talk to his brother after school.

But Arthur was busy with soccer practice and a piano lesson. When Stanley knocked on his bedroom door, Arthur said, "Just a minute." And a minute later, he said it again!

"I have a lot of homework," Arthur explained. But Stanley wondered if he had another reason not to talk. Did Arthur still think that Stanley was a cheater?

In school the next morning, Ms. Root called on

Evan to share his prediction.

"I think Stanley will go fastest," said Evan. "He is flat, after all. And he is light, like the pencil case. That's my hypothesis."

"Is that really a hypothesis?" Elena asked. "Maybe it is just a fact."

Her opinion was clear. "I think we all know that's what's going to happen. Stanley will slide the fastest because he is the flattest."

Ms. Root wrote the hypothesis on the board, using different words: "On the slide, a flat person will slide faster than a nonflat person."

When the kids went outside to run their first experiment, there was another class on the playground. It

was Arthur's class, having recess!

Stanley spotted his brother sneaking looks at the second graders as they got set up. He pretended he did not notice, though. He did not want to tell Arthur what his class was doing. He just wanted to show that being flat didn't mean he would always win. Being flat was not *magic*. No matter what some other kids thought.

Everybody watched while Stanley climbed to the top of one slide. "So who else wants to be in the slide-off?" Ms. Root asked her class.

Josie raised her hand, but Ms. Root chose Marco instead. Marco and Stanley grinned and high-fived as Marco climbed the ladder. Then they waited at the top of the slides.

"One . . . two . . . three . . ." said Elena, who was holding the stopwatch today.

They let go at exactly the same time! The sliding was so fast it felt like a blur to Stanley. But Marco got to the bottom first!

"That's strange," Stanley said.

"It's not what we predicted!" said Ms. Root. "Let's make sure it was not a mistake."

But when Stanley and Marco raced again, they got the same result. It was not a mistake at all. Flat Stanley came in *last*!

"I don't get it," Josie said. "What

happened?" She was pretty disappointed.

Sophia had an idea. "I think Marco is heavier than Stanley," she said slowly. "That makes him go faster. Like, a heavy thing will fall faster than a lighter thing, you know?"

Some of the kids looked at her blankly, so she explained. "One time my sister had to do a project for school," Sophia said. "She had to drop a book and a feather out of a second-story window at the same time. And guess what happened? The book fell faster!"

"I do weigh less than Marco," Stanley said. "Doctor Dan said I weigh just about the same as a pizza box!"

Ms. Root nodded. She said, "You have all heard of gravity, I know. The force of gravity brings objects down to earth. But heavy objects and lighter objects all fall at the same speed, even though it is hard to believe! The feather seems to be slower, though, because it can be picked up by the wind."

"Ooh! Stanley can be blown around in the wind, too!" Evan said.

"That is true!" said Ms. Root. "But now we have another question. Are gravity and air the only forces helping something slide?"

She was quiet for a few seconds, letting her words sink in.

"Maybe this one experiment does not tell the whole story," Ms. Root said, as if she was on the verge of solving a mystery. "Let's go back to our hypothesis: A flat person will slide faster than a nonflat person."

Elena raised her hand, even though she didn't need to. Out here on the playground, class time was more like a big conversation. "Does that mean *all the time*?" she wondered. "That Stanley will *always* go faster than a nonflat person?"

"Excellent question!" said Ms. Root.

Marco jumped in. "I mean, if we change some things about the sliding, something different might happen, right?"

Ms. Root gave him a silent cheer.

"You're thinking like a scientist now!" she exclaimed. "We need to put our hypothesis to a different test!"

"Yes, we need to do some more experiments," Josie agreed. She was still waiting for everything to work out the way she had expected.

Juniper added, "Okay. So we need to have a different setup. Remember when we wrapped the pencil case in plastic? Remember when we made the waterslides?" she said. "We need to change the slide . . . or we change the boys, somehow . . ."

Her voice trailed off, like she was not sure how to do that.

Stanley was not sure how to do that, either!

"So we send Stanley and Marco down a waterslide now?" Elena asked.

"We wrap them up in plastic?" Evan said.

Stevie jumped in right away. "No, that does not seem like a good idea," he said. "That would not be safe!"

It felt a little awkward, having everyone talk about him like this. Stanley was still standing right here!

"I have an idea," Stanley said, and no one seemed to hear him. He tried again, a little louder. "I have an idea!" he shouted. "I don't want to be wrapped in plastic or anything. But maybe there are some *other* supplies from the classroom that we can use to change the experiment?"

Ms. Root's eyes lit up. "Good thinking! Sometimes scientists must use their imaginations! I am sure we can find something that's just right."

For a few minutes, the class split into two groups. Ms. Root led some kids back inside to the classroom, while some other kids stayed outside, under the distant eye of Arthur's teacher.

While he waited, Stanley kept to himself. He sat on top of a set of bars, then flipped upside down on them. He was pretty sure that flatness didn't give him an advantage when he flipped! But maybe he would have to test it with science sometime!

When Ms. Root led his classmates

back to the playground, they were all grinning. They were carrying some things that Stanley did not expect— some snow pants and some jeans that looked big enough for grown-ups!

"It's time for a wardrobe change," Evan said. "And maybe, if you're lucky, a win."

More Experiments

"The snow pants and the jeans belong to a pair of twins who moved away," Ms. Root told her class. "The twins, Ben and Ken, left Maple Shade Elementary School when they were in the middle of sixth grade. And, once they were gone, teachers found lots of clothes left in their cubbies!"

"These clothes are perfect for us," said Marco. "Because they are exactly the same. And they are big enough for us to put on over our clothes!"

"It's a little too warm out to get bundled up," Stanley joked.

Still, he pulled a pair of jeans right over his own pants. They did not fit very well because he was flat and they were not. But he was ready to see the way they changed his ride on the slide!

Stanley and Marco climbed the ladders in their matching jeans. They sat on the top of the matching slides. They pushed themselves off the top at the same time. And not much happened! The jeans were stiff and rough. They slowed both boys down!

"I'm not even sliding!" Marco complained. He held on to the sides of the slide and pulled himself all the way to the bottom.

"I'm not sliding, either!" Stanley said.

"Hmm," said Josie. "You should be flying down that slide, since you are flat." She threw her hands up in the air. "Could you be doing something wrong?"

"No, no," Ms. Root said in a hurry. "No one is doing anything wrong. But the jeans and the slide don't fit together smoothly. There is a lot of friction between them because the fabric is rough."

"Friction?" asked Stevie.

"Think of it like rubbing, or scraping," said the teacher.

"Oh, I get it!" Evan said. "The jeans and the slide rub too much together."

Stanley got it, too. This was the opposite of what happened when he sat at his desk or on the bus! There was no friction then, he figured. That was why he was always slipping!

"Let's see what happens without a lot of friction!" Stanley called out. He was already putting on the snow pants. He had a pretty good idea of what was going to happen next. This would be his fastest trip down the slide!

The snow pants were shiny and superslippery. They slid right over Stanley's regular pants. When he walked in them, they made a swishing sound. And Stanley and Marco could barely sit on the slide in these snow pants! The minute they put their legs down, the snow pants carried them away. Marco slid so fast that he got all twisted up. He landed almost upside down at the bottom of the slide!

"Can we try that again?" Marco asked, laughing.

Sure enough, even when they sat down very carefully on top of the slide, the boys took off in no time.

Ms. Root whistled. She looked at the stopwatch. "Whew, that was fast!" she said. "Both of you beat your earlier times!"

And, she noted, the boys' times were closer together now. The slippery snow pants had made the difference in their weights less important.

The teacher led her class away from the slides now. She had the kids sit crisscross applesauce on the wood chips, almost as if this were an outdoor classroom. "We have a lot to think about!" she announced.

"I don't know what to think!"

Stanley admitted. His head was spinning. "We were supposed to be studying flatness. But now we are also studying gravity, and friction, and pants!"

The teacher smiled. "We have just done a lot of tests," she said. "We have seen a lot of results, too. And now we need to make up our minds about something. What makes a person go the fastest down the slide?"

Ms. Root was usually full of energy. She loved to talk and laugh. Now, though, she was quiet. She wanted her class to think.

Josie was the first one to speak. "Flatness," she said, though she did not sound so sure. "That's what makes a kid slide fast. Flatness always gives *someone* a head start."

Everyone knew which *someone* she was talking about.

"No, that's not right," said Juniper. "How can you say that? Didn't you see when Marco slid faster than Stanley? I think the weight of the person sliding is the most important. It's all about the gravity and the air, right?"

Juniper looked to Ms. Root for a reaction, but Ms. Root kept her face blank. So some other kids started talking, too.

Evan argued, "It's the friction! The less friction you have with the slide, the faster you will go. Didn't you see what happened with the snow pants?"

At that point, Ms. Root stepped in. "Let's remember our hypothesis, okay?" she said. "On the slide, a flat person will slide faster than a nonflat person. What do our experiments tell us?"

Sophia cocked her head. She was thinking hard. "It is true," she said. "A flat person can slide faster than a nonflat person of the same size. Like if they weigh the same amount, I guess."

"And?" Ms. Root prompted her.

Suddenly Sophia was not so sure. "Actually, it doesn't happen every time," she said. "So I guess . . . it depends."

Marco added, "A flat person has less friction with the slide, right? Because flat people are smooth? But flatness might not be enough to win every time. It's up to other things, too, like what they are wearing and how big they are. And how slippery the slide is! Like is it a waterslide, for instance?"

Stanley felt like he should say something. After all, he was right in the middle of this scientific question. He had a feeling his class was coming to the end of the scientific method.

"The hypothesis is true *sometimes*," he said. "Sometimes a flat person will slide faster than a nonflat person. And sometimes they won't. There are a lot of forces going on there. Flatness is only one of them."

"What matters is how flatness works with gravity and friction!" Elena called out.

Ms. Root was smiling now. Stanley could tell she wanted to give them the answer, but she wanted even more for them to figure it out on their own.

"So is our hypothesis correct?" she asked. "We need to come to a conclusion, based on our experiments. Is it yes or no?"

No one said anything.

If the hypothesis was wrong, then Josie was wrong. Stanley's flatness might have helped him win the swinging contest, but that didn't cross over into every contest. Being flat was not any more of an advantage than having long legs or big muscles. And Josie did not complain about those!

Stanley looked at Marco, and Marco looked at Evan, and Evan looked at Elena, who looked at Juniper, and on and on until the look went all the way around their circle—and Josie raised her hand.

"It is right a lot of the time," she added quickly. "Our experiments showed that!"

She took a deep breath. "But the experiments didn't always do what the hypothesis predicted," she admitted.

The whole class was waiting to hear what she would say next.

The room was quiet until Josie shook her head. "I can't believe it," she said. "But I guess the hypothesis is wrong!"

Conclusions

Stanley looked at the ground. No one liked making mistakes. And no one liked admitting mistakes to the whole class! He did not want to gloat.

But Marco was his best friend for a reason. He nudged Josie with his elbow. "Did you forget to say something?" he asked.

"If a flat person won't always win on the slide," she said, "then maybe flatness doesn't always help a person win at everything else, either," she admitted.

She did not make eye contact, but she muttered, "I'm sorry I said you cheated, Stanley."

Stanley was happy. But there was something else that he needed to say. And he caught up to Josie as they walked back into the building.

"I'm also sorry, Josie," he told her. "I mean, being flat did help me win the swinging contest."

"Yeah, I know," she said. She did not sound very happy.

"But that's not the same as cheating," Stanley explained. "It's just who I am! And being flat doesn't make everything easier. It even makes some things harder!"

Josie looked suspicious. "Really?" she said. "Like what?"

"Like sitting still," Stanley admitted. "I keep slipping out of my seat. It turns out there's not enough friction between me and the chair."

Josie actually smiled. "Is that why you get so many helpful reminders?"

Stanley did not want to be reminded of all his reminders. But he wanted to be friends with Josie, just like they had been before this all started.

"Being flat can even make it hard to fit in," he told her. "Because it makes me different from everyone else."

Josie seemed surprised. "I never thought of that," she said. "I don't always fit in, either," she told him. "I learn faster than the other kids."

"Really?" Stanley said.

Josie opened her eyes wide. "You didn't know? I might even skip a grade."

Okay, they were not different in the same way! But second grade would be better if they got along. So Stanley smiled.

"We can be different together," he said. And they could be friends as well as classmates.

Later that day, when his school bus arrived, Stanley climbed in and sat

in his usual seat. Arthur was in his usual seat, too, with his usual friends. From the front of the bus, Stanley could hear them talking and laughing. No one was talking or laughing with him, but at least Nate and Jaden waved hello.

Stanley had a bowl of cereal when

he got home. Then he went to the driveway to play basketball by himself.

He dribbled the whole length of the driveway before he took his first shot. He jumped and tried to dunk, but he missed the basket by a mile.

He dribbled in a circle and tried again, but his fancy footwork did not help. The ball hit the rim this time but tipped out of the basket. Stanley caught it before it hit the pavement.

He stood in the driveway with the basketball in his arms. He took a deep breath before he began dribbling again. Would he ever be good at this sport? Stanley wondered. A gust of wind could help him from time to time, but he needed more help than that. He wanted to know how to score when there was no wind at all!

Stanley thought he was still alone, so he was not guarding the ball. All of a sudden, though, someone raced around the corner of the garage and stole the ball right out of his arms. "Hey!" Stanley cried.

Arthur grinned. "You have to protect the ball!"

He dribbled in circles around Stanley, switching hands. He scooped the ball up and over his head, then caught it neatly with his other hand. He's showing off, Stanley thought sourly. His brother was acting just like Josie again.

Or at least that's what he thought at first.

"I'm sorry I called you a cheater," Arthur said as he tossed the ball neatly through the basket. "I know you can't help blowing away once in a while. It's not your fault, even if it helps you win."

He was right, of course, but now Stanley did not know what to say. "I definitely can't help it," he told his brother. "But science shows that flatness does not help me all the time!"

Arthur squinted at his brother. "*Science* shows it?" he asked.

"I can show you our experiments," Stanley said. "My class did some tests on the playground."

"Naaahh," said Arthur. "I believe you. Just show me your hook shot. We've got a lot of work to do!"

Arthur grinned again. "Because if flatness won't help you all the time, I'll have to help you. How else will you ever keep up with me and my friends?"

Try some slide science for yourself!

All you need is a slide, a friend, and a stopwatch. (You can also use a cell phone with a stopwatch function or app.)

First, find some small objects around your playground. Sticks, rocks, wood chips, even pine cones will work! Just make sure the items have different sizes, weights, and textures.

You and your friends can decide who will be the slider and who will be the timer!

The slider should go to the top of the slide with the objects. The timer can stay at the bottom of the slide with a stopwatch or a phone.

Then send the objects down the slide one by one, timing them as they go.

Which ones are fastest? Which ones are slower?

Remember, the force of gravity is always the same, but an object's speed will change depending on how much friction it has on the slide.

You can test this fact again and again! Try it with different kinds of balls: a tennis ball, a golf ball, a Ping-Pong ball. Try it with different kinds of shoes: a flip-flop, a sneaker, a dress shoe.

You can also build your own slides— or ramps—from cardboard or plywood. Objects' speed will change depending on the angle, or steepness, of the slide.

Who knew there was so much science on a playground?!?